I0538722

ESCAPE FROM PLANET FIDGET

Bruce Goldstein & Metin Sozen

HIGHLINE PRESS
70 Battery Place. Suite 822
New York, NY 10280
917. 532. 4227

escapefromplanetfidget@gmail.com
Visit: escapefromplanetfidget.com

Creator / Author: Bruce Goldstein
Creator / Illustrator: Metin Sozen

First Edition, September, 2017
Printed in the United States of America

ISBN: 978-0-692-94840-8

For all the kids in the universe.

ESCAPE FROM
PLANET FIDGET

ONE SPIN AND YOU MAY NEVER RETURN

Created by
BRUCE GOLDSTEIN & METIN SOZEN

CONTENTS

THE DISAPPEARANCE OF DAREDEVIL DANNY

Danny was the first to go.

Three weeks ago he was playing fetch with his chocolate Lab Bosco and he never came home. I wasn't there when he disappeared, but he told me everything when he returned. Brace yourself. I hardly believed it myself.

His name was Danny Walker, but he was known around the schoolyard as Daredevil Danny. Nobody could spin a fidget like him.

"Spin! Spin! Spin!" His fans would cheer him when he spun the Nose Propeller and the 8-finger Power Popper. And Danny loved the attention. But that day, Bosco didn't care about his fancy spins. He just wanted his master, not

"the Fidget Master," to throw the gooey green tennis ball.

"Woof! Woof! Woof!" he barked.

"Okay boy," Danny said, throwing the disgusting ball to the other side of the playground. Thirty seconds later, he was back, ball in his mouth, panting for another round.

"Well that was fast Bosco," he said. "Now try this one on for size. Go get it boy!"

But this time, after Danny threw the ball, he told me he heard a buzzing sound. And when he turned his head around, he spotted something glowing and spinning under the swings.

He said he didn't know what it was, but he felt the need to walk over to take a closer look at it. And when he bent down, he was sure glad he did.

"Coooool!" he said, as his eyes widened.

It was a silver fidget spinner, and it was spinning so fast that it was making blue, green, purple and silver rings. He told me it was so beautiful to look at — a rare gem of the street— and he wished I was there to see it. Danny said that it looked like it had been spinning forever.

Since nobody was around to claim it he picked it up and started doing tricks — well, half of a trick. Once the Daredevil leaned back and had it spinning on his forehead, Bosco came barreling into him causing the spinner to hit

the ground. *Clank!*

Danny was very frustrated. "Bosco, bad dog!" But he had an idea. "Okay boy, you want to play, huh?"

Bosco went nuts. *"Woof! Woof! Woof!"* Yeah! Yeah! Yeah!

Well, Danny wanted to play too except with the shiny fidget. So he wound up and threw the ball over the fence, into the weeds.

"Go get it boy!" he said, feeling a bit guilty. And Bosco took off like a bandit.

"That'll keep him busy for about 15 minutes," he said to himself.

"Now, it's spin time. Starring me, the one and only Daredevil Danny. Oh, yeah!"

He did the Tilted Head Forehead Spin, the Wrist Wrap Around, and the Under-the-leg Dagger! And as the fidget spun faster and faster, and the colors intensified, he felt the urge to take a closer look. He told me he felt it calling him near. And it really did. Because when Danny looked more closely, the purple and blue pigments swirled around and around, and his pupils spun in circles. He went into a deep hypnotic trance. Then, suddenly, the spinning stopped and the fidget dropped onto the pavement.

Clank.

When Bosco eventually came back with his silly dog grin and drool spilling down his chin, he must've been surprised to not see Danny. The furry guy must've been sad and confused. *M'mmm. M'mmm.*

The next morning Danny's mom and dad found Bosco sleeping next to the fidget. He spent the whole night staring at it, waiting for his master to come back from wherever he went.

Things didn't look too good until a few days later when a little girl with a lot of spunk got involved. And that little girl was me. This is my story.

FIDGET FEVER

Hi, my name is Lila Gallagher. I'm 11 years old and go to PS119. I'm a bit of a nerd, so if you need me, chances are you'll find me and my nerdy glasses in the library. I always play it safe. I wear a helmet when I scoot and I carry an umbrella just in case. And you know what? I like it that way. But when those ridiculously annoying fidget spinners appeared, everything changed.

It was like one day they just showed up out of nowhere, like they just dropped from the sky. Blue ones, purple ones, yellow ones, sparkling ones, glow-in-the-dark ones, camouflage ones, superhero ones, and even ones that played pop. They were buzzing around my school like a swarm of rainbow bumble bees. Kids were doing tricks on the front steps, under the flagpole, in the yard, and even in the classrooms. You couldn't walk a block without seeing a kid trying to spin one on his thumb or forehead. They were crazy about them. *Cuckoo crazy. Obsessed!*

My mother said it was just a fad. "You'll see, it's just like a Hula-Hoop or Slinky."

I had no idea what she was talking about. But she was wrong about this. I was in the thick of it. Trust me, I got hit with a red one in the neck during home room.

Even the smart kids got sucked in. Jack Marley, the honor student, said that he knew that they were stupid, ridiculous even, but he admitted that he just couldn't stop spinning. "I'm addicted," he said.

But that wasn't me. Give me a break! I couldn't believe everyone was being brainwashed by a bunch of jellybean-colored ball bearings. I had a billion things to do with my time other than spinning a silly top, like read a book, code a video game, work on my science experiment, or paint my toenails.

Monday was my favorite day at school. Mathematics and Chemistry. But that particular Monday, we had interrogations. Big time. A bunch of detectives with mustaches were snooping around the school, interviewing us about the disappearance of Danny. They were doing it one by one in a closed room. The cops were just as flustered as Bosco.

As for Danny's fans, they put up MISSING SPINNER posters around the neighborhood: HAVE YOU SEEN THE DAREDEVIL? REWARD: 10 FIDGETS.

It was a sad day at PS119. Everyone's parents were worried sick, thinking it could be their kid next. And for three mothers and fathers it was. Juggling Jackson disappeared outside the supermarket. Hot Potato Henry vanished by the movie theater parking lot. And Big Stack Jack disappeared by the bike path. The only things that could possibly tie the cases together were the fidgets left behind. But the police still hadn't taken the idea seriously.

It was very hard to concentrate in class, thinking about these missing kids. We all just stared at each other, thinking the same thing. Who's next? The day just dragged on and on. I painted a tree in art class. I did a few equations in math. And after I almost blew my face off in chemistry, the clock struck 3 and everyone headed for the door.

Sandy, my trusty scooter was parked outside. After I secured my helmet, I stepped on, pushed off, and headed to the library. I was on a mission for knowledge. That helped me relax. But before I even left the school property, I heard my name being called. "Hey Lila. Look, over here!"

When I turned my head to see who it was, I almost crashed into a lamppost. Surrounded by a bunch of troublemakers was a tall kid with blue eyes and spiky hair. He was on a skateboard, balancing 6 fidgets on his body — one on his nose, one on each ear, one on his chest and one on both elbows. A real showoff. He was also my real brother — twin brother — Luka. They called him the The Spin Master. He was the best spinner in the whole zip code. Even better than The Daredevil.

"Hey watch this sis!"

"I'm watching." *Boring,* I said under my breath.

Somehow the Spin Master was now walking on his hands with spinners on his feet.

"Pretty impressive, I guess, if you can't read."

"Hah, hah, Lila," Luka said. "Can you please help me with something tonight?"

"Sure, whatever" I said. Then I got on my scooter and hit the road.

"Bye Nerdy, Nerd," he said, upside down with a spinner on his nose.

"See ya later Freaky Fidget. And be careful. In case you haven't heard, Fidget Kids are disappearing."

"Sure, sure. You be careful, too."

"About what?"

"Reading, ha, ha, ha. Your brain may explode!"

As I scooted away, his smelly friends bounced around and grunted like animals.

THE KID WHO COULDN'T SPIN

Luka and I were different in so many ways. Aside from being born on April 8th it was hard to believe we were related. He was cool and popular. I wasn't. I was smart and witty. He wasn't. And I was good looking. And he was a monkey butt, with breath that stunk like a skunk.

One of the few things we did agree upon was our mutual disgust for mom's meatless meatballs.

"Dinner time!" my mother yelled to me and Luka upstairs. "It's meatball night!"

"Oh great. Gross," we moaned.

Since we couldn't tell mom we hated them, we secretly made silly faces, holding our necks like we were being poisoned. We would've given them to our lazy bulldog, Lilo, but even he wouldn't go near them. He ate them once and got a nasty case of doggy diarrhea.

Fortunately, on nights like this we had a stash of Halloween candy. After we excused ourselves, we made our way to the front stoop where we split a monster-sized, crunchy chocolate bar for our main course, followed by a pack of rainbow juice busters, and a grape lollipop for dessert.

It was such a beautiful night. Thousands of stars were out. We could see The Big Dipper, Orion, and Cassiopeia. What a light show!

"So Luka, what do you want to ask me?" I said under the constellations.

"Well, I need some help with my book report."

"What else is new?" I snickered.

"So will you help me?" he asked. "It's on *Lord of the Flies*."

"Yes."

"Awesome! You rock, sis!"

"Not so fast, mister," I said. "I want you to teach me a fidget spinner trick."

"Wait, is this a trick? You hate fidgets. You despise them."

"No, I'm serious," I said. "I thought I might appreciate them more if I could actually spin one. Plus, I'm sick of kids making fun of me. I want to be cool like you."

"Listen Lila, even if I do decide to teach you one, it's not like it's easy to do."

"Yeah, but you're Spin Master Luka," I said. "Nobody can teach me like you can. Don't you know you have the most awesome moves?"

He didn't even know I was tricking him with flattery.

"Well yeah, I guess I do."

"So let's do it, Master Luka. Let's spin!"

"Ok, now let's start off slowly with the Convertible," he said, handing me an orange fidget. "That's the cool move Toe Finger Wellington taught me."

"Cool," I said, trying to sound hip and confident.

"Now, watch and learn. I want you to place the spinner between your thumb and middle finger and start spinning with your left pointer. Once you get it going, release your thumb and start balancing.

I tried it for about 15 minutes, and I was getting very, very frustrated. He kept telling me that I could do it.

"Have patience, sis."

Then, after my 40th try, I lifted my thumb and it was finally spinning on my finger.

"Like this? Like this?" I asked and smiled, all excited.

"Exactly. You're doing it," he said.

"This is actually pretty cool!"

Once I got a taste for fidgeting, I wanted to learn more. He wasn't up for it, but when I told him I'd tutor him in math, he taught me four more moves: the Change Up, the Reverse Sonic, the Polarity Switch, and the Sidewalk Leapfrog.

After I practiced awhile and realized that I needed a lot more practice, I told him to teach me the best one for fun.

"I want to be a Master," I said.

He started laughing. "A master, huh? A master of what?"

"What's so funny?" I asked.

"I don't want you to get hurt. Or me. You didn't hear what happened in school today, did you?"

"Hear what?"

"Scott Lawson got a fidget in his eye."

"That explains the patch."

"Teach me," I insisted. "Or I won't do your report Piggy."

"Who's Piggy?"

"He's a main character in your book report."

"Okay. Now don't say I didn't warn you."

He led me to a splintery, wooden telephone pole and said, "Listen, carefully."

"All ears, Master," I giggled.

"Now the key to this trick is to complete it in your mind before you even begin. It's about visualizing. You need to connect with the spinning power in the universe and visualize a positive outcome."

"What's it called?"

"Shhh!" Suddenly so serious. "It doesn't have a name. But when you master it, you will hear the fidget whisper, you'll feel tingles down your spine, and you'll know you've arrived. You will spin from within."

"You know... you sound crazy."

"Not crazy. Confident, positive, a believer," he said. "Just know your goal, see it achieved, and believe in yourself."

"I only believe in myself when I'm taking a math test."

"Well, I believe in you, even if you're a bookworm."

"Thanks bro."

"Okay, let's do this," he said, pulling out a fidget necklace he'd been wearing. He shuffled through a bunch of colors and picked out an orange one.

"Let's use this," he said. "I won it off Fast Fingers Frankie from Oakville."

After we selected the fidget, he etched a little X on the pole and had me stand 20 feet away.

"Okay, now focus and hit the mark."

"Are you serious? That *X* is so tiny. And I'm so far away."

"You wanna be a master? Be cool?"

"You really think I could be cool?" I asked.

"Throwing the fidget would be a good start."

"Okay, here I go." So I took a deep breath, and just when I was about to throw it, Luka put a green camouflage blindfold over my eyes.

"No way," I said. "Are you crazy?"

"This is the only way."

So I focused, took a deep breath, and saw my orange fidget stuck in the little X on the pole. Okay, I visualized.

Then I took my shot. *"Doh!"* Right in the weeds. The second time I hit a mailbox. *"Doh!"* And the third time, I almost hit a cat.

"I stink so bad," I said.

"You just need practice. Try other moves like the Sweet Potato, and work your way up to the Ninja Banana Spinna.

"How long will it take?"

"Some can train forever and never get there. But you have Gallagher DNA like me, so maybe a master is waiting to come out of you, too. And once you do, you can control fidgets with your mind. No hands. Do a bulls-eye 20 feet away. You'll have power — Even more than me. Well, maybe. Hah, hah."

It was getting late, so we headed in.

"Hey Luka, here's your fidget back."

"No, it's yours. I'll win another tomorrow," he said, putting the orange spinner around my neck.

"Maybe I'll win one too," I smiled.

"Maybe you will sis," he said. "Maybe you will."

We fist-bumped and went to our rooms. I put on my headphones and dreamed of fidgets all night long.

LOST IN THE LIBRARY

The next day at school, there were so many fidgets spinning around, it seemed like they had quadrupled overnight. It was a fidget epidemic. One fidget was no longer enough to fill my classmates' spinning needs. Mark Melito had 20, Vicky had 14, and Hudson had 9. It had become a serious problem. They weren't just preventing kids from focusing and learning. They were distracting the rest of the students too, even geek brainiacs like me.

Although I had fun spinning with Luka, the buzzing and battling on kids' desks was driving me coconuts. I couldn't concentrate to take a test. I actually got a math equation wrong! Simple algebra. I was really fuming. One time I was sitting in the cafeteria and, out of nowhere, a spinner came spinning down the table and into my mashed potatoes. It was like I was a target. They didn't mix well in science either. Tommy Smith dropped a rainbow fidget into a chemical and it caught fire.

The bathroom was by far the worst. The mischievous Mulberry brothers created a game called DROP THE SPINNER AND FLUSH. As you can imagine, it created quite the mess for Vinny the janitor.

One day, after tons of teachers' complaints, and after someone shoved a green fidget in our principal's tailgate, he made an announcement over the loud speaker: "ATTENTION STUDENTS OF PS119, FROM THIS DAY FORWARD...

"Class, please stop talking and listen," Mrs. Bonzak said. "Principal Hardybutt is speaking."

"She said, "BUTT," Eddie said. And the whole class was cracking up.

... FIDGET SPINNERS ARE FORBIDDEN. THEY ARE BANNED. ANY FIDGET FOUND WILL BE CONFISCATED."

Sad faces all around. Kids booed. It was like they took away tablet screen time. Me, I was lucky, because I really didn't care. Take away my science kit, and I'd punch you in the nose, but fidgets, who really needs them? I felt bad for Luka though. He really loved those things. He was actually good at something.

The best. Ever since we were kids our parents never supported him in anything. But I always stuck up for him.

"You're the best, bro," I'd say.

"Thanks sis."

"Wonder Twins forever," we said fist-bumping together.

Well, Mr. Hardybutt wasn't kidding. Ten minutes later, a big box with a diagonal red line going through a fidget showed up in class. Of course, Luka's collection took up the most space. Because no matter how many spinners Mrs. Bonzak took away, he brought another one in the next day. He just kept winning them at street spin-offs after school.

After a week, he was driving Mrs. Bonzak nuts, so she threatened him. "Luka, either stop bringing those things in or you're going to do serious study time after school."

"That wouldn't be cool," he said.

But Luka just couldn't resist showing and telling his classmates about his winnings. When he defeated Speedy Spanky by Willy's Deli, he spun his hi-tech spinner onto Olivia Martin's desk. But when it spun onto the floor, it made a loud clanking sound and the fidget exploded. Dozens of ball bearings scattered everywhere, causing Sharon Levine to trip and almost crack her head open.

The class was cracking up, and Mrs. Bonzak flipped.

That was it.

"Mr. Luka Gallagher, you are to report to the library, 4 – 6pm, for the next 2 weeks."

"That's after school," he yelped.

"Yes it is," she said. "Miss Rosen will be expecting you."

The library was a foreign place for my skate rat brother, so I walked him down the hallway to show him around.

"So you're Luka," a pear-shaped woman in thick glasses and three chins said. "So are you ready to study?"

"Thrilled," he said, with a big grin.

"Stop being a wise guy," I told him and sat him down at a long table with my fellow bookworms: Melanie, Penny, and Alice — clearly not the crowd he was used to hanging with.

After I handed him two books to read, "ENGLISH IS COOL" and "ARITHMETIC: MORE THAN TERRIFIC," I split. Forty minutes later, the doorbell rang.

Ding. Dong.

"Melanie, what are you doing here?"

"It's Luka. He disappeared from study time."

"Figures. He was probably bored and just left."

"Not quite," Melanie replied.

Melanie was usually a calm vanilla cookie, but I'd never seen her freaking out like this. Her glasses were steaming up.

So I told her to sit down and take a deep breath.

"Ok, *huh.* So after you left he put down the math book you gave him, and he started flipping pages in every other book on the table. He couldn't focus. Luka's head looked like it was about to explode from boredom. That's when he bent down to tie his red sneaker and came up with a yellow fidget. He let out a sigh of relief and starting spinning it around the table. It was very annoying so everyone got up except me. Then he asked me if I'd like to take a spin."

"So what did you say," I asked.

"I said, "I—Don't—Spin," and he kept on doing it. Faster and faster and faster, and then when it started glowing and making purple, yellow, and green circles, he picked it up for a closer look. And that's when it happened. His eyes grew wide, his jaw dropped, and he said, "Co-ooool." And then I couldn't believe my eyes — I still can't ..."

"What? What happened?"

"He got sucked in. First his face, then his neck, and then the rest of his body. The only thing left was the fidget glowing on the table."

"That's crazy talk. He probably just snuck out."

"Trust me. He didn't."

"What about Miss Levine?"

"She was snoring in the corner."

When I couldn't take the insanity she was feeding me, I asked her to leave. Then I went out front to suck on some sour snake candy.

I couldn't believe my best friend was crazy. I mean, disappearing into a fidget was totally insane, but it wasn't like Luka to disappear for that long. With no calls, no emails, no texts, no smoke signals, I sensed something was very wrong. We were twins after all. *"Luka, where the heck are you?"* I said. *"Come home bro. You're scaring me."* And that never happened. Except when he jumped off the roof into McMillan's kiddie pool.

It felt weird sitting out front on my own. Just last night he had placed that fidget necklace around my neck. Well, that night I swore I'd never take it off until the day I become a Spin Master like him — which was more likely never. But hey, with my brains and my natural Gallagher DNA, anything was possible.

As the moon appeared, I put my face in my hands and dropped my face down to my knees. Suddenly, tears slithered down my cheeks. "Luka, where are you, you goofball?" Then I felt a presence.

"Luka, is that you?" But it smelled like swamp water and stinky farts. And there before me, were the dirtiest sneakers I'd ever seen.

WEIRD KENNY

When I looked up, I saw who the fat farty sneakers were attached to. A stocky kid with pig tails on the top of his head, and big bug eyes. If I hadn't seen him around school, I would've run for my life. They called him Weird Kenny. He was the new kid. He had just moved here.

"You scared me," I yelled. "What do you want?"

"It's actually what *you* want?"

"I doubt it."

"No, trust me, it *really* is."

"Just leave me alone. My brother is missing."

"I know."

"What do you mean, you know?" I said. "How could you

possibly know that?"

"Because I know where he is."

"You do?" My ears perked up. "And how in the world is that possible?"

"Because they took me there, too."

My eyes grew wide.

"*They*? Whose *they*? And where are *they*? And where is my brother?" I asked. "Is he close by? Please take me to him now."

"That's not possible," he said shaking his pigtails. "Not yet. If you want to know more about getting him back, come to my tree house tomorrow night."

"*Hmmm.*"

I had to think about that invitation for a minute. They didn't call him Weird Kenny for nothing. *Ah-hee-hee-hee-ha!* He laughed like a crazy spotted hyena. He never came to any social events. He talked on a walkie-talkie without having any friends. And the kids made fun of him.

"*Weird Kenny. Weird Kenny. You're a Weirdo.*," they would chant to him at recess.

But you know what I say about that. I take "weird" over "bullying" any day of the week. So I figured what do I have to lose — besides my life — and I brought along my brother's slingshot in case I needed to take his eye out. I'm serious too!

One time, I shot a raccoon in the butt while it was eating garbage. Big mistake messing with Lila Gallagher.

"Okay, Kenny, I'll do it, because I know Luka would do the same for me.

"That's *marvelous*," he said, laughing away. "*Ah-hee-hee-hee-ha! Ah-hee-hee-hee-ha!*"

I just had one issue meeting him at the tree house. I had no idea where it was. Nobody in town did. They said he lived with animals deep in the forest.

When I asked for a map, he laughed, "*Ah-hee-hee-hee-ha!*" Not in a million years. You'll never find it."

"What about my dad's GPS?" I asked.

"Useless. Just meet me at the playground on Redgrave, by the broken swing at 9:09pm on the nose, wear loose clothes, a hairnet, thick boots, put on a lot of bug spray, and bring an 8oz. jar of dill pickles."

"Are you kidding?" I asked. "Pickles?"

"Do you wanna see Luka again?"

"Okay, 9:09 it is."

"*Ah-hee-hee-hee-ha! Marvelous!*"

Ouch! I almost woke my parents up when I snuck out my window. But I was on a mission: to get my goofball brother back.

I showed up right on time at the swings, wearing green sweatpants, a hairnet, and ladybug boots, armed with a jar of dill pickles. *Now where was the weirdo?*

"Boo!" he jumped out holding a flashlight up to his eyes.

"Man, you scared the *heebie-jeebies* outta me."

"Sorry, I couldn't resist. It's my sinister look! *Ah-hee-hee-hee-ha! Ah-hee-hee-hee-ha!*"

"Here," I said, handing him the dills. "So where to?"

He pointed to a hole under a tall metal fence.

"Follow me," he said, "and don't look down."

"Oh great."

As I sunk into a foot of sludge, got bitten by crazy bugs, and got poked in the head with sharp branches, that explained all the stuff I brought along (not the pickles, though).

As we went deeper and deeper into the woods, and heard howling, I feared getting eaten or lost, so I listened for Kenny's creepy laugh *"Ah-hee-hee-hee-ha! Stay close Lilahhhhhhhh,"* and it kept me going.

Except when he thought he was being funny.

"Watch out for the snake!" he screamed, and I jumped.

"Just kidding *Ah-hee-hee-hee-ha! Sorry Lila.*"

"You dork."

"Sorry, I really am."

"Are we there yet?" I asked.

"Almost. Did you put your bug spray on?"

"Uh oh!"

"Well, you might want to cover your arms, legs, neck, and close your eyes, and your mouth."

"When?"

"Now! And don't mind all the slimy slithering things

moving below."

"I'm not falling for your snake tricks again."

"This time, I'm not kidding. *Run Lila, run... Ah-hee-hee-hee-ha! Ah-hee-hee-hee-ha!*"

Oh, man. There were thousands of mosquitos buzzing in my eyes, around my lips, and up my nose.

Ow! Smack! Ow! Smack! Ow! Smack! I screamed, and swatted them away.

"Well, we made it!"

The sign on the tree trunk read: "Rotanipsdrol."

"What in the world does that mean?" I asked.

"Who knows? It was there when I got here."

"Now Kenny, what's the reason you brought me here?"

"Oh, oh, you'll see, Lila, you'll see," he said, pointing to a rope ladder. "Just please take off your swampy boots before you enter *Ah-hee-hee-hee-ha!*"

I didn't know why I had to take my boots off until he swung open the door, and my jaw dropped. Coooooool! It wasn't a tree house. It was a super secret lair — a luxurious, high-tech, cool-castle library up in the air. And there was a green rug. I thought I was dreaming. This strange kid had everything — from an awesome tablet to a large screen for movies and playing video games. He also had tall shelves filled with books ranging from the complete Harry Potter Library to Gardening 101. He also had test tubes filled with green goop, silver alien models, dinosaur fossils, a magic wand, and a life-size skeleton.

"Holy moly," I pointed. "Check out that telescope!"

And when I looked up, he had solar paneling. Man, he could probably see Uranus. Your *anus*. That was a joke between Luka and me. Ah, it's not the same without Luka.

"Kenny, this place is incredible," I said. "Where did you get all of this stuff?"

"My Grandma. She's loaded. She invented crazy glue. She's crazy as a bat. But she always sends me birthday money. Sometimes twice a month, sometimes three."

"Lucky dog."

When I asked Kenny where he lived and where his real house was, he told me he lived with his Aunt Milly, about 1 mile north of his lair. But he said he spent most of his time there. Who wouldn't? He even had a waterbed in the corner and a solar dish for the Science channel.

The place was a dream. But there was one thing that I didn't understand: the mice. So I asked him, "Kenny, what's with all the mice in the mazes? You must have over 100."

Kenny's eyes widened and gave me a mischievous grin.

"Ahh, you haven't met Veronica, the lady of the house yet," he said.

Then I heard a hissing tea kettle. *Hsssss.*

But it wasn't a kettle. Holy moly! Kenny reappeared with an 8-foot anaconda around his neck. The snake's tongue licked his cheek. Yuck.

"That's a good girl," he said.

If that wasn't sick enough, he dangled a squirming mouse's tail from his mouth and let Veronica devour the rest of it. I almost barfed.

Then he asked me to dance.

"You wanna what?" I asked. He was getting weirder by the second. And then he pointed to the floor that I was standing on.

"Well, not exactly dance. More like spin."

When I looked down, I realized I was standing on a large spinner board (Luka practiced on one in our basement.) But it didn't make sense. Kenny didn't have any spinners. *So I thought.* When I heard some type of buzzing above my head, I looked up.

Wow! This weirdo was full of surprises. There were over 100 fidgets, maybe more — blinkers, stinkers, and medieval slicers (I had read about those in my brother's comic books) — hanging down from the ceiling on individual nylon strings, about 10 on each one. It looked like they were floating and spinning like planets in outer space.

Looking around, Luka would've loved it here. Then I got really sad, remembered what I was doing there in a tree house in the middle of nowhere, and jumped up and said, "So where is he?"

"Who?"

"Stop being funny. Where is my brother?"

"Okay," he said. "Now I want you to relax and sit crisscross applesauce."

"Are you serious?"

"Yes. You want to find Luka? It's necessary."

"Okay, so I got into position and sat across from him. Then, as he was about to begin whatever he was about to do, he let out the loudest and stinkiest FART ever. I mean a real whopper.

"What's wrong with you?" I shouted. "You stink!"

"Pickles give me gas."

"Then why do you eat them?"

"Because they're *sooooo* tasty."

"Well, you're gonna poison me with your toxic butt breath," I said.

"Whatever. Now pay attention," he said, unclipping a

rainbow blinker from above his head. "Now, whatever you do, do not look too close at it. Not yet."

"And whatever you do, don't fart again," I said.

"So one night I was out back, catching muskrats to make yummy muskrat pie ..."

So gross.

"...when suddenly I saw something glowing on a rock, so I took a closer look. It was a florescent green fidget spinner. It looked like it had been spinning for hours. And since nobody was around, I brought it home."

"Then what?"

"Well, I spun it, and watched it go. But this green sucker spun faster than any fidget I had ever spun before. There was no limit, so I gave it all I had. I spun it around and around and around. I spun it on my nose, my elbows, and on every bone in my body, until I felt this spiral glow drawing me near. And I couldn't help but stare into it. And that's when I saw it."

"Saw what?"

"It," he said. "There was something moving within the florescence, far off in the distance. And it was just marvelous. *Marvelous!* I couldn't stop staring. And the more I stared into it, the more I felt myself getting sucked in. This magnetic force took over suddenly and I was thrust inside a tunnel of colorful light, a vortex of some type, and then, and then ..."

"And then what?"

"I came out of the other side."

"Other side? Where in the world was that?"

"Far, far away from this world. It was so crazy. One second I was sitting here crisscross applesauce, and the next second, I was running in a circular tunnel — with an unbalanced floor — with hundreds of people, aliens and wild creatures yelling RUN, RUN, RUN! Since I had no idea what everyone was yelling about, I kept on running and running, which really wasn't good for me, being that I have asthma and left my inhaler back at my treehouse. I lose my breath just thinking about it."

"Aliens?

"Yes."

"Like little green men?"

"More like 6 arms and fangs."

"Did you know where you were running to?"

"No, but I knew we were running from something — something not too friendly."

"How did you know that?"

"Because every time we ran around the tunnel, I heard people and aliens screaming. And when we came back around, many were missing."

"Oh my gosh, did you see Luka?"

"No."

"What do you mean, *no*? Then why am I here? How do you even know he is alive?"

"Because I heard two guards — fidget fighters, they called each other — talking about where he was staying: Area 1600. That Luka was one of the leading contenders in The Intergalactic Spinner Olympics, and that Lord Spinator was very impressed with him. That he may be the Golden One."

"What in the world are you talking about?" I asked, shaking my head. "Golden One? Lord Spinator? You're talking crazy talk."

"No, I'm talking about Planet Fidget," Kenny said.

"Well you certainly watch a lot of space movies," I said, "and you have a wild imagination, but you expect me to believe all that jibber jabber?"

"No. But you have to," Kenny said.

"Okay, let's suppose this nonsense is true. How in the world did you get back Kenny?" I said sarcastically.

"Well I was just getting to that. While everyone was running, I spotted a giant spiral vortex going the opposite direction that I came in, so I took a chance and jumped in."

"Then what happened?"

"I felt myself going around and around and around and I visualized my treehouse. Then I transported back to Rotanipsdrol and the first thing I did was eat a juicy dill pickle."

"Pickle, huh," I said. "Well, Kenny, that's a great story, but I wish you had some proof about Luka."

"But I do," he said, grabbing his tablet. "Pull up a stump." And then he offered me some chocolate milk, dried figs, and a pig knuckle.

"Just give him a chance," I told myself. *"Do it for Luka."*

INTERGALACTIC SPINNER TRACKER

Since I was going to be there a while — and had no idea how to get home — I munched on a garlic dill. I prayed it didn't give me gas like farty boy. I also guzzled gallons of chocolate milk. Good stuff.

To set the mood, Kenny set up a battery-operated campfire. After a couple of marshmallows his big eyes glowed from the orange embers. "Okay, now listen carefully," he said. "So I was back home from this crazy planet and since nobody was going to believe me I decided to figure out what was going on on my own. Why were they taking kids? Why certain ones over others?"

"Keep going, keep going," I said.

"Well, I started with the obvious route: I checked out the serial numbers on the boxes that the fidgets came in. And lucky me, I noticed there was something different and yet similar about the serial numbers:

089 6111 SP3N4   089 6112 SP3N4   089 6113 SP3N4

Each box had the same numbers, except for the 7th digit. So I went online and explored the secret side of the Internet to see if I could find some answers, some dark site where other kids who had been taken by aliens exchanged information. And I did. I hacked into The Intergalactic Spinner Tracker (the IST). It was a highly sophisticated tracking system set up by aliens on Planet Fidget. They used it to abduct human beings for reasons I did not know. It was pretty impressive, I must admit, but there still wasn't any real proof. Then he gave me the biggest grin — lots of green teeth — and pointed to his screen. There was an image of the universe. Now see all those blinking fidget like shapes?"

"Yeah."

"Well, those are the kids being taken this very moment."

Kenny saw my jaw drop and eyes widen. I got a chill.

"Believe me now?"

"Uh, huh." I think I drooled.

"Good. Now watch this. I'm gonna zoom in on that green planet with blinking white lights."

"What's that?" I asked.

"More like where's that?" he said, smiling. "Planet Obotaki, and that lime green creature is an Obotakian."

"Nuts. Well, can you see my brother?"

"Yes, I can go back a day on Earth. I record them so I can rewind all of the previous fidgetuctions if I need to. Like now."

"Holy, moly!"

There he was, Luka was being sucked into a fidget in the library. Melanie wasn't lying.

"Cool, huh?"

"So take me to him," I said.

"Yes. There's just one problem."

"What?"

"He may not want to leave."

"What?" My face dropped now.

"Just something I heard," Kenny said.

"I'll explain when we get there."

"So can we go now?"

"Absolutely not," Kenny said. "You need 48 hours of

vigorous training. We need to get your energy up, and get your spinning up to speed. Because if you don't get selected, you'll never get near him. Remember, Lord Spinator has his eyes on Luka. He could be the Golden One."

It sounded completely crazy, but Luka was my bro. So the next 2 nights, I snuck out to train with Kenny. We started off with the basic spins — the Thumb Spin, the Knee Topper, and the Potato Bopper. Then Kenny moved me up to the Kung Fu Spineroo. Now, that was a toughie. I had to stand on my left foot, put a silver gear spinner on the tip of my right shoe, kick it, snap it back, and when it popped up, catch it spinning on my thumb. We also dueled to the Fidget Edge and battled like true fidget warriors. My favorite was the Knuckle Sandwich. I had to spin fidgets on all ten of my knuckles. When I made my left and right hand touch, the fidgets flew everywhere.

"That's just marvelous, Lila!" he said *"Ah-hee-hee-hee-ha! Ah-hee-hee-hee-ha!* You are now ready to find Luka."

"Ew," I said. "What's that smell?"

I looked at Kenny.

"Sorry."

RUN!

I was so nervous. This was outer space we were talking about. Plus, I was scared of Kenny. I mean, really, where was this weird kid taking me? After he dimmed the light, we sat down on the spinning board, crisscross applesauce.

"Ready?"

"Now move closer to me."

So I moved closer.

"Just a little closer now."

"Hey, wait a second. Are you trying to kiss me? Is this what this is all about?"

"No way, yuck," he said. "Listen, if we're not close, we can end up on different planets in the Universe. Trust me, Uranus is no picnic. It really stinks."

"It sure does," I said, smiling.

"Okay, time to get serious," he said. "Now pay attention."

He rolled up his sleeves and placed the fidget on his sausage-sized index finger. Then he gave it a spin. And then when he got it going really fast, he said to put my thumb over the fidget and to apply pressure.

"Faster, faster, faster," he said. "SPIN! SPIN! SPIN!"

So I spun like a speed demon and together we were really cooking. Round and round it went. We were vibrating. The tree house was shaking like a blender. And then I looked into the fidget and watched the rings change colors, from red to orange to yellow to magical pigments I'd never seen before. *Sooooo* beautiful. The swirling tunnel of colors looked like a pinwheel or a ginormous lollipop. As my mind spun around in circles, I spotted something glowing in the distance. There were little figures moving around. I wanted to touch them so badly so I stretched my arm forward.

"No, not yet," Kenny snapped, yanking my arm back.

"Kenny, what's that?" I asked.

"Just focus," he said, humming. "We're almost there."

Then, out of nowhere in my mind's eye, I saw a dark image. I felt chills, and I wanted to turn back, but then I saw a flash of Luka. He wasn't himself. So I knew I had to stay the course. *Luka, I'm on my way.*

"Now, remember, the second you arrive," Kenny said. "You need to RUN, RUN, RUN! No time to think, or it's over. You're over. There are no second chances."

"Okay, got it," I gulped, and I kept spinning. More pressure. *More pressure.*

The last thing I remembered before we arrived was staring into the glow. We must've gotten sucked into it because now we were inside of it, running like maniacs.

"RUN, RUN, RUN!" everyone was yelling just like he said. It was a stampede. It was hard to believe that just moments ago, we were sitting in a tree house and now we were running on an unbalanced floor — a giant spinner I thought — trying not to fall. And we were far from alone. There were hundreds of kids our age from all around the universe running for their lives and we were all in shock.

"WHERE THE HECK AM I?" I wanted to shout, but if I stopped, I was going over. To where? Who knew?

Then, if things couldn't get any crazier or wackier, I got whacked in my neck by a sharp stick. When I turned to my right, I learned it wasn't a stick. It was the tail of an 8-eyed kid. And when I turned to my left, there was a tiny little red guy with teeth on top of his head.

"RUN, RUN, RUN!" everyone kept screaming as they climbed all over each other to get away from what was coming up from behind them. No idea what it was, but it had horns, and it was flinging green goop everywhere. People and creatures couldn't run fast enough, and they were trampling over each other. Many fell off the edge. Their screams faded as they fell farther and farther into an abyss.

Kenny was having a hard time keeping up. He was huffing and puffing and out of breath. "I forgot my inhaler again," he said.

"RUN KENNY, RUN!," I shouted. "KEEP UP! TAKE MY HAND! TAKE MY HAND!"

"I'm coming. I'm coming," he said.

I was in the worst nightmare ever.

"RUN! RUN! RUN!" everyone continued to scream. "SHREEEK, SHREEEK, SHREEEK!" Aliens screeched like nails scratching a blackboard. And then I felt something wrapping around my feet, and then licking me. When I looked down, I regretted it immediately. It was a giant orange snake with three tongues. I felt like I was gonna pee in outer space.

And then, as I was running, Kenny yelped. He was really out of breath. "Huh, huh," he panted. "If anything should happen to me, make sure you're picked. Keep your energy up. Go for the gold! Go for the gold!"

"What are you talking about? You're not going anywhere. I don't know where to go."

"You'll be fine! You're a Gallagher!" he said.

Then, I heard him scream, a scream that echoed forever. I would've felt sad, but I had to stay focused. I was on a mission to rescue Luka. So I kept RUNNING AND RUNNING AND RUNNING until the giant silver spinner we had been running on suddenly stopped. And there was silence. And there were only six of us still standing on the platform. Five kids just like me, except they had fur, antennas, and fins. But no matter what they looked like, or where they came from, we were all scared, out of breath, and wondering what happened next.

While we were waiting for somebody or something to tell us what the heck was going on, we chatted it up and got to know each other.

BEEEZLEY introduced himself first. He was a 400lb beast with 6 arms. He was the quickest dirtiest spinner on Babalonia because he had 6 trick arms and never took a bath. But his bright smile made up for the stench.

SMARTINA from Inteligenzia had one of biggest brains in the universe. She was a non-stop thinker. With all of her mind power, she had the ability to solve any situation 92 times faster than any being in the galaxy.

MONTY was a mind-reading monk from Martakon. Whenever his moods changed, his horns changed colors like a chameleon. He could spin with the best of them without lifting a finger, and could predict his opponent's next move.

PHOOEY was a fish-faced creature from Lavania, one of the seven water planets. When he opened up his rubbery mouth wide, he could spin three fidgets on his tubular tongue inside.

FLEXIA was from Metamorphica. She could take on any form. From human to falcon to rubber band to glue stick. No limits. All she had to do was focus, and she would become it.

And then there was me: LILA, the loser. I told them I was here on a mission to find my brother. I told them about Kenny. But they didn't believe me. At least these guys were friendly.

As different as we were, there were two things we had in common. We were all kids, and we were the best spinners back where we came from.

Suddenly, there was a loud slap that echoed throughout the dome. SLAP! SLAP! SLAP!

I looked left to right, and then I saw dozens of creatures up above, looking down on us. They were chubby little guys, really little, shorter than me, with three eyes. And they didn't have feet. Say what? They had thin, little frog legs attached to fidget spinners.

"Hey Monty," I whispered. "Look, they have fidget feet." *Dreaming. Definitely dreaming.*

They didn't walk. They spun — some faster than others. My new space buddies referred to them as fidgeteers, and the name stuck.

There were three slightly larger ones on the balcony. The one in the center looked like the leader. He was covered in fidget-shaped medals: a purple, a yellow, and two gold. He spun forward to look down at us. Then came the introductions.

"Greetings, children of the galaxies. My name is Captain Frank. Welcome to Planet Fidget."

"Hey, what are we doing here?" Phooey shouted. "Why did you take us from our homes?"

"Not take you. Borrow you. Now please let me continue."

We all nodded, and listened intently.

"Okay, guests, the reason that you are standing here is because the 6 of you have shown us the skill, the strength, and the energy to make it through the Unbalanced Axis Challenge."

"Yeah, well what happened to the others?" Monty shouted turning beet red.

"We sent them back home," Captain Frank said.

"Well I want to go home too," Beeezly shouted.

"Me too," Flexia said.

"But what about our parents?" Phooey said. "They're going to worry about us."

"Don't worry. You'll be home before they even realize it. You're in a different time zone. A very different one."

Just as I was about to ask about Luka, he said, "Enough. No more questions. Lord Spinator will tell you everything tomorrow." Then he pointed to his top two fidgeteers: Mobi was a boy with two curls, and Mali had flame-shaped hair.

"Please take our special guests to their charging stations," he said.

"Yes Captain," Mobi and Mali said at the same time, and they spun down a ramp to greet us.

"Mobi me, pleased to meet you," he said in a human, robotic voice.

I was terrified and giggling at the same time.

"Mali me, pleased to meet you," said the other one.

Charging stations? Kenny never said anything about that. But he never made it this far. Now I was totally alone. And where was Luka? The worst part was that even if I found him, I had no idea how to get us home.

Mobi and Mali instructed the six of us to climb aboard a circular board with wheels.

"Now hold on. I hope you don't get motion sickness,"

Mobi said, laughing.

I felt like a piece of luggage as they rolled us around and around through the busy city. Everywhere we looked, things were spinning. The roads were spinning. The buildings were spinning. Birds were spinning. And of course, all of the fidgeteers were spinning. After Mali dropped off Beeezly, Mobi showed me to my quarters.

"Lila, your personal pod," Mobi said. "Sheila awaits to make your acquaintance."

"*Oh man, I'm not sharing a potty in my pod with any alien,*" I said talking to myself out loud. "*Besides, how do these fidgeteers even go potty? I can't even imagine.*"

Mobi overheard me and said, "You just put your booty on the poopaway and say, bye, bye stinky."

I really wished Luka was there. He would've been laughing his butt off.

When I entered the pod, there was a robot at the door — a long, thin, metallic female robot with a high-pitched voice. It was good to see somebody else with long legs, but what was with the long roll of silver fabric she was holding?

"Lila, meet Sheila," Mobi said, yawning. "Take good care of her, Sheila."

Then, like a vacuum, he went into a corner and attached a hose from his belly button to a charger, and he was out. Now it was just Sheila and I.

The whole experience was crazy. I felt like I was the star of a sci-fi movie.

"No need to be scared little earthling," the robot said. "I bet they tell you crazy things about outer space beings."

"I'm not scared."

"Okay, so just lay on the table, and close your eyes," Mrs. Roboto said. "Relax."

There was a lot of pushing and pulling, and I had no idea what this tin can was doing to me. I felt like I was getting wrapped in silver masking tape. And then, the moment I'd been waiting for — she spun me out of my cocoon to look into the mirror. I was terrified to see what that hunk of junk did to me. But when I looked into the mirror, I couldn't believe it. I was wearing a sparkling silver suit. *Whoa, mama, did I look cool!* I was now Lila Gallagher the Superhero.

"Oh silly human, you haven't seen anything," Sheila said. "Now lay down again and don't move. It's time to install your spinergy sphere."

I didn't even ask. Since the silver costume was pretty cool, I left my eyes open for this. I was glad I did because of the crazy light show about to happen in my skintight silver suit.

"Now beware. You may feel a light shock or a sting, but don't worry, it can't hurt you. Well maybe a little."

"What!?!" I jumped.

"Just kidding, earthling," Sheila said.

"Beeeeeep!"

"Hey, that tickles. And look, I'm blinking different colors."

"Ka-kool," Sheila said.

"So what's this suit all about?" I asked.

"Just close your eyes, sleep on your back, and tomorrow you'll find out. Good night, human."

"Good night."

FIZZY POP

That night, I lay in bed. My head wouldn't stop spinning. Around and around I went. I felt so lost and confused, but I knew Luka was near. Then I heard a knock at the door, and I stuck my head outside the circular window to see who it was. Holy Moly, it was Beeezly, Smartina, Monty, Phooey, and Flexia.

"Come out and have a fizzy," they all said.

"Hey guys, what time is it?"

"Well, it seems like there isn't any time on this planet," Monty said.

"So we might as well have a quick fizzy at the FizzyPop," shouted Phooey.

"Are we allowed to go out?"

"*Hmmm.* Well nobody said we couldn't."

I looked in the corner of the room and saw Mobi charging. Busy day.

"Okay, one fizzy."

When we walked into FizzyPop, we were the tallest beings in the place. Red and green and yellow fidgetmen looked up when we walked in. Maybe it was our matching silver suits.

When we stepped up to the fizzy stand, Beeezly ordered up a round of fizzies—because that was all they served. They came in a 3-inch high cup and only 2 flavors: SCHLUEY and WECKLER.

Schluey was freshly-squeezed, exotic meat juice with a twist of zapo. Weckler was a rich blend of blue cork, maple syrup, and a tincture of red weckler leaf. The guys got Schluey. I went with Weckler. Tasted okay, but my pee was purple, and smelled like cherry bubblegum. Note: next time, order Schluey.

That night, we talked about life on our planets, cool spinner tricks, and why and how we were all brought together.

I broke the ice.

"Well, I guess this proves there is life on other planets."

"Hah! Hah! Hah!" We all laughed, grunted, or shrieked.

"I knew it was true!" Flexia said.

"I knew it too!" "Monty shouted.

"Well, we're all aliens to each other, I guess," I said. "Until we meet and become friends."

"Well said Lila," Smartina said, smiling.

"Yeah, and who would've thought we all had fidgets in

common," Beeezly added.

"I miss spinning back home," Flexia said. "I could throw a fidget 20 feet up in the air and then stretch myself up in the air to catch it."

"Pretty cool," Monty said. "But can you make six spinners spin in midair without touching them?"

Everybody cheered, "He got you beat!"

"Oh yeah, well," Phooey said, "back on Lavania, I could spin fidgets on my tongue and then spit them out one by one, landing on a cone."

But that night wasn't all about showing off our skills. Things got emotional, too. Beeezly opened up about how he was on his own since 3. He said his parents wouldn't keep him because he was too large and had 2 extra hands."

"It's alright buddy," Monty said, "you're with us now, wherever we are."

There was a moment of silence, except for the loud music coming out of the speaker near our kneecaps. Then something very weird started happening. I felt this blast of energy flow around inside of me. My chest, toes, fingertips, neck, and mind were pulsating. I couldn't stop moving. And I was talking really fast. It must've been the fizzy, because all of my alien pals were also acting peculiar.

"FIZZY RUSH!" we all screamed. And we all started dancing. Then while we were bopping around, something cool happened in the center of the FizzyPop: Bumper Fidgets. OMG! 12 banged-up fidget spinners started smashing into each other. *Bang! Smash! KaBoom!* It was awesome. I was laughing and making howling and screechy sounds with my new buddies. Before we left, we toasted in a bunch of languages.

"Cheers! Bandiatoa! Eeechala, Zolpa! Kaidox! Lavitat!"

We had no idea what time it was, but we figured someone would come looking for us soon. What we didn't know was that somebody knew exactly where we were all along. When I turned my head to the left, I saw Mali watching us. I don't know why, but I didn't tell the guys.

SURVIVAL OF THE SPINNIEST

The second I opened my eyes, I popped out of bed like a toaster tart. Mobi was hovering over me, and he had the worst breath, like rubber and cheddar cheese.

"Dude, what are you doing?" I asked. "Don't you brush?"

"Time to rise," he said.

I didn't know where he was taking me, but I looked good! The power sphere on my chest looked like it was part of me. I was like Iron Girl. It beeped, and I lit up like a robot.

"This is nuts," I screamed. "Here I come to save the day! Someone's day!"

"Nuts? Mobi no understand." Then, he smiled and said, "Let's go. Ball wait for you."

"Ball?" I said.

"Yes, ball," he grinned.

Mobi rolled me onto a round ball bus with no bus driver. It was spherical, like a giant pinball.

"Good luck," Mobi said.

Now that scared me. What do I need luck for? I just sat there alone, rolling along, listening to some awful pop spinning song. DOOT! DOOT! DEET! It was driving me insane. DOOT! DOOT! DEET!

When I went to yell to shut it off, nobody answered. Great, we were running by remote control. But then it stopped, and a big beast got on. It was Beeezly and he had the same blinking lights coming out of his chest like me. "Looking good, buddy." Then the other guys boarded, too. "Hey Lila! Hey Monty! Hey Phooey! What's up Flexia?" We called each other THE SILVER SIX.

As we rolled around the city, we were all getting antsy. Beeezly was rocking back and forth. I felt that he was going to barf beans on everybody. Finally, the sign on the ball bus lit up: THE SPINARIUM, NEXT STOP. So we spun around in a circle, rolled down a ramp, and it just let us out in front of a huge stadium. I felt like we were going to see the Super Bowl or World Series. But this wasn't that kind of sport.

And it seemed that whatever was going on inside, we were the star attraction. We heard cheering from outside the wall.

Before we could enter, we had to pass the Frenergy detector. There was actually a big sign that read: FRENERGY DETECTOR. It was a little tunnel, where the fidgetmen waved a red blinking stick over our power spheres to see if we were running on the right frequency. We all passed, but I really wished I didn't.

As we entered, I looked up and almost fell down. There were over 100,000 fidgeteers in the Spinarium. Three tiers up. All different colors, sizes, and sounds. There were also black and white fidget fighters wearing red helmets, holding metal sticks twice the size of them. There was chanting that sounded like thousands of bullfrogs burping in harmony. There were also yellow fidgeteers spinning around, delivering refreshments. Everywhere I looked, there was some form of entertainment. There were blue aliens doing acrobatics and dog-like creatures fetching spinners. There was also a Spinerician pulling a slimy green alien out of a hat. So ridiculous! Then, the mood changed. The fidgety guards led us to the center of the arena and had us sit in a circle — backs against each other — so everyone could observe the aliens. The main attraction — us.

As the fidgeteers FOOOOED and BOOOOED, suddenly,

I heard a jet coming towards us. It was getting louder and louder. And then the whole Spinarium chanted:

SPIN-A-TOR!

SPIN-A-TOR!

Then somebody yelled, "Look there he is!"

Where? We looked left and right, and then we heard it hovering directly over our heads. When we all looked up, there was a long-legged being in all black, hovering above our circle of silver suits. And then in one powerful demand, he shouted, "SILENCE," and silence there was.

"HELLO FRIENDS FROM ACROSS THE UNIVERSE. THANK YOU FOR COMING. I AM LORD SPINATOR."

"HUH, HUH, HUH." He sounded like an astronaut in a space mask, gasping for air.

"I GUESS YOU'RE ALL WONDERING WHAT YOU ARE DOING HERE. ALLOW ME TO EXPLAIN."

As he spoke, he appeared on large screens everywhere. It reminded me of an evil villain, announcing his takeover.

"RECENTLY, OUR ENEMY, THE ROCKTAVIANS, HACKED INTO OUR SECURITY SYSTEM, KNOCKING OFF OUR FIDGET FORCEFIELD, WHICH GAVE THEM ACCESS TO OUR SPINERGY RESERVE.."

His face got closer on the screen. *Ooh scary.*

"...THEY STOLE 87% OF OUR SPINERGY, LEAVING US WITH BARELY ENOUGH TO KEEP US SPINNING ON OUR AXIS. ON MY AXIS..."

That explained the wobbling.

"...SO IF WE DON'T RESTORE OUR SPINERGY

SOON, PLANET FIDGET WILL DRIFT FAR, FAR AWAY TO A DIFFERENT TIME AND SPACE..."

I was dying to know what mumbo jumbo would come out of Lord Poopitor's mouth next.

"...SO WHERE DO WE GET THE SPINERGY TO HELP PLANET FIDGET?"

Let me guess.

"YOU."

Oh goody. I felt privileged.

"...BECAUSE YOU ARE THE BEST SPINNERS IN THE UNIVERSE. AND DUE TO YOUR EXTREME SKILLS, YOU HAVE THE MOST SPINERGY...

What was he talking about? Dude, speed it up. And "SPINERGY?" Give me a break. Just say "energy."

"...HOWEVER, CHILDREN OF THE UNIVERSE, THIS IS NOT ENOUGH. WE NEED TO RAISE IT EVEN HIGHER..."

I was afraid to ask how. And I should've been.

"...BY COMPETING AGAINST OTHER SPINNERS IN THE INTERGALACTIC SPINNER OLYMPICS."

Oh great. I just couldn't imagine where the masked man was going with this.

"EVERY TIME SOMEONE WINS A BATTLE, YOU TAKE THE LOSER'S SPINERGY. AND AFTER 3 LEVELS,

THE SPINNER WITH THE MOST SPINERGY WILL GET A CHANCE TO GO FOR THE GOLD — TO REACH THE GOLDEN TOWER FOR FOREVER TREASURE."

Hah, hah. That had to be the most ridiculous thing I had ever heard.

As Lord Spinator was talking our ears off, I looked at my new friends. We all looked at each other. Was this some mean trick to introduce us and then put us in the ring to tear each other apart? That was really mean. I thought about whom I would have to fidget fight with. I loved Beeezly, but he'd kill me.

"Hey, when can we go home Mr. Lord Spinator?" Monty shouted, waiving his arms.

"WHEN WE HAVE ENOUGH SPINERGY," he said. "BUT BY THEN, YOU AND YOUR RAINBOW HORNS MAY WISH TO STAY HERE FOREVER."

"Forever." That's what weird Kenny had warned me about: "Beware Lila, Luka might not want to leave."

I was yet to understand what would make these kids want to stay in captivity with this spinning buffoon.

Before Lord Spinator spun away, he shouted so loud that the planet vibrated: "FOOOOOOOOOO!" Then the crowd screamed their little fidgets off. "FOOOOOOOOOO!"

"ARE YOU READY?" Spinator yelled.

"FOOOOO!"

"ARE YOU READY?!"

"FOOOOO!"

"EXCELLENT. I WILL SEE YOU ALL VERY SOON. *"MUAHAHAHAH!"* He laughed. And poof, he was gone.

I was trying to make light of it all, but the reality was that I was a prisoner on another planet. And nobody knew where I was, except for Kenny, and he fell into that abyss. He meant well, but he got me into this mess.

My buddies looked worried. Beeezly looked defeated. Monty was trying to go to his happy place. Flexia and Phooey were fearing for their lives. Smartina was counting. None of us wanted to fight. Especially me. I came here for only one reason — to get my brother back — and nothing was going to stand in my way.

When Mobi and Mali put us back on the silver bus ball, they brought us the best news of the day — none of us had to fight each other. Thank goodness.

But they also brought terrible news. In order to make us strong and take our spinergy, they were going to put us up against the strongest, meanest, ugliest, most experienced spinners in the their solar system.

Oh, rats!

LET THE SPINNING BEGIN

LEVEL PURPLE:

LADY AMAZONIA vs. TINY LILA

I was terrified about my first battle. The closest thing I had ever competed in was the spelling bee. I spelled "comprehensive" correct and won with flying colors. But this was different. This was physical. I had to do tricks, outsmart my opponent, and be ready for anything. I'll never forget when the fidgetmen spun me into the Spinarium, and thousands of fidgeteers BOOOOED down at me. It was horrible. I missed my friends. And when Lord Spinator looked dead center at me I got a chill down my back and almost barfed all over my shiny new suit. Then came the war drums.

FA-FOOM! FA-FOOM! FA-FOOM!

My heart was beating like crazy when I stepped up to the platform. I was terrified. All the FOOOOING didn't help. Well, I love you, too. I threw a little sarcasm back at them.

I still wasn't 100% convinced that this wasn't a dream, but when a fidgeteer threw a can of green slime at me, it was hard not to believe. All I could do was face up to who or what was about to join me in the ring. I had to be strong. Beyond strong.

"Oh my gosh." I almost passed out when I saw my PURPLE opponent. I was doomed. Captain Frank introduced us. LADY AMAZONIA vs. TINY LILA.

The moment she stomped onto the platform, it was clear to me that this lady was not a lady. She was bald with a dragon emblem on her purple shirt. She had a scar where her right eye used to be, and she was covered head to toe with armor like a great warrior. *Oh great.* I felt like I was going to die. And when she pulled out a spear, I almost pooped in my pants. Nobody said anything about spears. So it was just me and my nerdy glasses.

"FIDGETS READY?" Captain Frank asked. "POWER SPHERES SET?"

We both said, "Yes."

"COMMENCE SPINNING."

Then, without warning, the floor started opening and closing, and I almost fell in. What the heck was this?

"That's where you're going," Lady A said. "Get back here you baby earthling." Then she spun 6 fidgets on her spear and lunged them towards my chest.

"Stop, that's gonna hurt."

"No, this is gonna hurt," she said, pointing to the open and closing floor. No way. No abyss for me. I'm from Earth you mean freak. Then I had an idea. As she was poking me, I ran up her spear, jumped onto her head, and did a 12-fidget smack down on her shiny dome.

"Take that, dragonlady. I'm Tiny Lila. I breathe fire on you. POO! POO!"

The crowd went wild. FOOOOOOOOOOO! LILA!'"

Then as luck would have it, there was a hole in the floor neither of us saw coming and into the abyss she went.

"Yay! My first victory," I said. "Now who's next?"

It had been a very long day and I was back at my pod on the poopaway. I was reading a very cool Spinny magazine. Suddenly, I was interrupted by a loud garbage truck coming down the street. But it was actually Mali on a supersonic chariot spinner coming to get me.

"Tiny Lila, Lord Spinator awaits your presence."

"Are you serious? It's so late."

She was serious. So I flushed, and it almost sucked my whole, skinny human butt down the tube.

As I climbed aboard, Mali said, "Now hold on."

"Why?"

"This is why!"

She spun me down a silver ramp at like a million miles per hour. Headed for a mini mountain, I had no time to brace myself. "Nooooooooooooooo!," I screamed.

Then just in time, secret doors in the mountain opened automatically and I spun right up to Spinator's feet. He smelled so familiar. *Sniff. Sniff.* But I just couldn't place it.

"SO TINY LILA, ISN'T THAT WHAT THEY ALL CALL YOU?"

"Not my choice."

"WELL MY TINY EARTHLING, YOU REALLY SHINED TODAY. YOU REALLY PUT THAT DRAGON 'POO POO' FACE IN HER PLACE..."

"Thank you, that means a lot coming from you, Lord Spinator," I played along with his ego.

"...AND NOW YOU RECEIVE YOUR REWARD."

"You never said anything about rewards."

"IT'S MY WAY OF SAYING THANK YOU. YOUR NEXT BATTLE IS IN 2 DAYS, BUT NOW YOU MAY DO WHATEVER YOU PLEASE ..."

What was the catch?

"...YOU CAN PLAY FOOKIE, MAKE SATURNIAN SPORES, RIDE FIDGIEBOARDS, EAT FUNKY SPANDY, OR DO WHATEVER FLOATS YOUR LITTLE SPACESHIP. JUST ASK MY RIGHT OR LEFT HAND FIDGETEER: MOBI OR MALI. THEY'RE HERE TO ASSIST YOU."

"I want my brother back. That's all."

"YOUR BROTHER?"

"Luka."

"OH LUKA. HE IS SPINNING HIGH UP IN THE SPOCKER LEAGUE. NEARING THE GOLD, I HEAR. HE IS ALSO A WISE GUY. ALWAYS MAKING JOKES. THAT KOOKIE LUKA ..."

Sounded just like Luka. I felt good knowing my brother was alive.

"...WELL, THE ONLY WAY YOU CAN SEE LUKA IS IF YOU COME IN FIRST IN THE MAXIMALO LEAGUE, AND THEN SPIN AGAINST HIM TO GO FOR THE GOLD TO REACH THE GOLDEN TOWER..."

"That sounds pretty impossible," I said.

"...WHY, NOT AT ALL, LITTLE GALLAGHER. YOU MAY BE STRONG ENOUGH TO BEAT HIM, BUT NOT GUARANTEED."

I had no interest in going to any gold tower. But this was my shot at saving him, even if I had to drag him by his ears or kick his skinny butt back to earth.

When I looked up to say thank you and good night, he was gone, but little Mobi appeared.

"Hi Mobi. I wish you could speak in complete sentences

and tell me what's really going on here." And then Mobi smiled and said, "Oh, but I can Lila."

I was so excited. He told me that all wasn't what it seemed to be on Planet Fidget.

"You are being tricked by Lord Spinator," Mobi said. "It's all lies. *Lies. Lies. Lies.*"

"I knew it," I said. It was about time someone stepped up to tell me what the heck was going on. Even if he spins.

"Mobi, please tell me everything."

"Yes, but not here," he said "It isn't safe."

Then he spun me down the hall to a red bean bag and told me a story. So we didn't look suspicious, Mobi got us some Mars burgers, Venus candy, and a jumbo pitcher of Weckler Fizzies.

"Okay," Mobi said. "Now pay attention." And that's just what I did. "It began 3,000 years ago — long before the war of Sargo and Lethalma."

"What's Sargo?"

"Not important. It's backstory. Now listen up ," Mobi said. "It was when Planet Fidget became part of the starry Spinnila solar system."

"How did that happen?" I asked.

"Listen, and you'll find out."

"Sorry," I said, nodding okay.

"The elders say it was a collision of three stars: Marca, Salma, and Formica. When they collided, a large mass formed Planet Fidget."

"So that's why there are three sides?"

"Exactly," he said, nodding. "But Captain Frank can tell you everything. He was there. He saw it all. Just catch him at the FizzyPop and buy him a few Wecklers. He'll chew your Earthling ears off."

"So what about you?"

"Not much to tell," he said. "When our parents died in the Great Battle of Pontapagus, Captain Fidget raised me and my sister."

"Sister?"

"Yes, Mali."

"Wow, I can see your fidget feet, same color."

"Mali and I were close as fidgies. We're twins. Just like you and Luka. Back then, our planet had been lacking SPINERGY so Captain Frank sent out a team to find the most energetic creatures in the universe.

When they landed on Earth—hundreds of years ago— the Spinergy Scouts stayed invisible to observe the inhabitants: humans. They watched and waited. Days turned into weeks and weeks into years. Then, one day, they spotted him in a playground. He was a young boy on the swings, no more than 10. They watched him kick his legs higher and higher. He had such a wide smile, bright green eyes, so full of life. And then, in broad daylight, the Spinergy Scouts beamed him back to the ship. They named him Energivios.

When the ship took off into the sky it left a huge Tri-circular design in the cornfield. It was the shape of our fidget ship — what your people refer to as crop circles. It's funny that you, and your fellow earthlings still don't know if these circles came from alien ships. Hah! We've been leaving fidget circles all around the universe for centuries. Maybe you should tell them it's true when you get back home?"

"Home?"

"We'll discuss later."

"So when Energivios first arrived, he made spinergy for the planet and the Captain was pleased, but it also made Energivios have more energy, which made him more powerful — even more powerful than Captain Frank.

Then one day, all the spinergy got to his head, and he snapped. He dressed in all black, put on a mask and became Lord Spinator. Some loved him, others feared him, and no fidget fighter was brave enough to fight him. Me, I never

trusted him, but Mali did. She became his lying little spy — little fidget butt kisser."

"So how old is Lord Spinator today?" I asked.

"Hard to say," he said. "Hundreds of years old, at least, and he can take any form. Over the years, we've invaded many planets, so he could appear as any of the inhabitants. All we know for sure is that there once was an Energivios. They took him from his home and stole his youth. And once he got a taste of spinergy, he FINALLY LOST HIS MIND."

"Wow, sounds like a cool movie."

"Child, this is my reality," he responded. "So what you see before you is a lie. You cannot trust him. The rewards are just incentives to keep you going, getting stronger, gaining more spinergy to give to him. HE'S POWER HUNGRY. He wants to BE RULER OF ALL TIME AND SPACE.

"What about the Gold Tower?"

"There is no golden treasure tower," he said sadly.

"Well, what about the thousands of kids he sends home?"

"Do you really think someone named Lord Spinator sends anyone home?" he said. "Who do you think is holding this planet up? Kids who fall in the abyss. He uses their energy to hold up the three sectors of the planet. But it's not enough.

That's why he created the Intergalactic Spinner Olympics."

"So what do I do?"

"You have to win. WIN. WIN. WIN. So you can get closer to Luka, knock some sense into him, and escape."

"How can we escape?"

"Leave that to me."

Just then, we heard a sound, and I saw a dark shadow.

"Shhhhhh, it's Mali," he whispered. "She mustn't see you with me. Go now, Lila."

"Thank you, my friend," I said. In a wink, he was gone.

LEVEL BLUE:

TINY LILA vs. DJ SPINTEROID

Just because I won the purple level, I was still worried about what crazed maniac they would have me spin up against next? And then I heard pop music fill the Spinarium, and broke out in laughter. This time, I wasn't spinning against a Spinner. I was spinning against a *real* spinner. A DJ with high-tech headphones inserted into his eardrums. What was he gonna make me listen to? 80s music from Mars? Beats me. Besides, I won Purple already. This should be easy-peasy. When Captain Frank announced us: TINY LILA vs. DJ SPINTEROID, the crowd went wild. They FOOOOOOOOED their fidget feet off.

"FIDGETS READY?" Captain Frank said. "SYNERGY SPHERES SET?"

We both said, "Yes."

"COMMENCE SPINNING."

More like commence "dancing." But I quickly learned Earth DJs were different than the ones in Fidgetland.

"OKAY, LET'S DO IT. LET'S DO IT. LET'S DO IT!"

And he did it.

DJ Spinteroid started spinning some super-sized fidgets with his tiny hands. That wasn't fair. The judge didn't seem to care. And when he got his spinner up to speed, he made music and hot jams shot out of his sound system. It was deafening.

EVERY FIDGET IN THE HOUSE, GET CRAZY. GO CRAZY. GO SPINNY. SPINNY POP. SPINNY POP POP!

He was killing me with funky beats. Pretty impressive, I thought, but not as impressive as my shoulder blade bop.

"Take that!"

We were going point-for-point until out of nowhere this giant robot rose up from the center of the disc and— OMG — started shooting colorful paint pellets at us. They were coming at us a million miles an hour. I was covered. I looked like a bag of rainbow candy. Too bad it didn't taste like candy. "Yuck!" But I was still zigging and zagging, dodging them. I was rolling and jumping, and spinning spinners on my head, and the robot went wild and shot hundreds of paintballs all at once. It just happened to be right where DJ was standing.

SPLAT! SMACK! WHACK. SPLAT! SMACK! WHACK. SPLAT! SMACK! WHACK!

By the time the robot got finished splatting him, DJ looked like he got pooped on by a thousand pigeons that ate Skibbles for lunch. I didn't look so good myself but, hey, I won. One more level to go.

LEVEL GREEN

TINY LILA vs. ROCKTOPATAMUS

When I entered the ring, my opponent was nowhere to be found — until I felt drool drop on my head and looked up. Holy Hippobutt! 400lbs. of it. This fat monstrous octopus with furry tarantula arms was un-suctioning itself to join us. And when he moved, he left a trail of slippery sludge. I gulped and felt my tummy rumble. This was gonna be really ugly.

When the Captain announced us: TINY LILA vs. BIG, BAD ROCKTOPATAMUS, the crowd went wild.

They FOOOOOOOOED!

"FIDGETS READY?" Captain Frank asked. "SPINERGY SPHERES SET?

But then something happened. We were interrupted by the sounds of heavy, deep breathing. *HUFF, HUFF, HUFFING.* It was so intense and haunting that everyone in the Spinarium felt it. It gave me chills on the back of my neck.

When it passed, the match began.

"COMMENCE SPINNING."

Now, I must say, for a 400lb. octopus with a furry hippopotamus butt, this beast could sure shake his booty. Within seconds, he had a fidget spinning on each of his 8 hands. Since I only had two hands, there was no way I could top that. I was stumped. Then, another obstacle appeared. Suddenly, the platform transformed into a vertical climbing wall with red blinking spinners as handles. And if you couldn't spin and hold yourself up at the same time, down into the smoky, fiery abyss you went.

The fact that the sun kept shining in my eyes didn't make things any easier. Then I had an idea. Sometimes being nerdy comes in handy. While the monster was taking a bite out of the platform, sliming all over the place, I took off my glasses, aimed one lens at the light, and the other into his big eyes. SCORE! He let out such a HISS, like a 400 lb. lobster boiling in a cauldron. With him temporarily blinded, I had a chance to make a move. But what move? Ah-hah! I stuck his arms together with sticky fidgets, and he couldn't do anything about it, except shake his fat jowls and fling goop at me. Suction sucker!

What a plan. Luka would have been proud of me. Well, I wasn't through yet. While he was whining, I climbed up to spin the winning spinners. And then, when the hairy fellow tried to stand, he fell through the floor. BYE! BYE! FATSOPOTAMUS!

I hope they had room for his big ol' butt down there. The crowd went wild. And they announced the winner: me. AND THE WINNER OF THE GREEN LEVEL IS TINY LILA FROM EARTH! SHE WILL BE THE ONE GOING FOR THE GOLD."

FOOOOO-LILAHHHHH! "Yes! That's me!"

That evening, Mobi and I went over to FizzyPop and ordered Spaceboogers, Marshmallows, Asteroid Pops, and we watched Spaceflix. First-class Fidget living was pretty good, but I wasn't there to play. I asked Mobi if he had seen the rest of my buddies. His eyes saddened as he said they were in sector 144B.

"Where's that?" I asked.

"It's the draining station. It's where the losers go.

It's where Mali transfers their remaining energy into Lord Spinator's spinergy sphere. He has so much now that he is becoming a power monster."

"Oh no. What can I do?"

"WIN, and you can save everyone. Be a hero. We believe this is your destiny. It's in the prophecy. It says that one day, a girl will come from another galaxy and free all the kids and fidgeteers living in captivity."

"Well, I don't know about that," I said, tugging at my orange fidget around my neck. "But I'll do my best."

As we kicked it back and enjoyed our spinny snacks, Mobi whispered, "Now everything is set. I have the way to get back. But you have the hardest job: to make Luka see the truth and get him to follow you."

"I can't wait."

"Now remember after the battle, meet me at the fidget fountain, and I'll help send you both home, okay, just —"

Suddenly, he put his finger to his lip, "shhhhhh," and pointed. It was Mali.

"Mali, what brings you to FizzyPop?" Mobi asked. "Just getting a weckler?"

She just smiled. The spy. She heard everything, which meant Lord Spinator would soon too.

LUKA vs LILA
LEVEL GOLD

I couldn't believe I was finally going to see Luka again. I just hoped — despite what anyone said — he was as excited to see me, as I was to see him.

Before I even entered the Spinarium, I heard the thunderous roar of fidgeteers: "GOLD! GOLD! GOLD!" And when Mobi spun me inside — holy moly! — I couldn't believe my eyes. There was gold everywhere.

There were over a fillion fidgeteers, and they were wearing golden clothes, whacky gold wigs, and sporting their gold-plated spinners for this special occasion. There was also a fidgeteer conductor in a gold suit, leading the intergalactic fidgeteer orchestra. *FOOM! FORP! FOOM FORP!*

And up on top, there were a bunch of fidgeteenagers, banging golden poppers and spraying gold silly string all over the place.

As the anticipation grew, everyone threw hundreds of golden fidgets in the air. They spun around and around. Very cool — as long as they didn't hit me in the head.

And then came the fireworks. FA-FOOM! Fillions of golden sparks. An explosion that rivaled the 5th sun of Soria. So bright, my parents could probably see it on our stoop through the vortex.

"GOLD! GOLD! GOLD!" they chanted. "SPIN-A-TOR! "SPIN-A-TOR! "SPIN-A-TOR! They longed for their leader. Then out of nowhere, their Master appeared.

"Look up!" a fidgeteer shouted. They all pointed above. And there he was in his jet black, jet-powered hovercraft. He spun around in circles, leaving a golden trail of smoke, and parked 50 feet in midair. Unlike the other levels, this time he sat very close to the action, 10 feet from the ring so he wouldn't miss a thing. Neither would Mali, the evil snake sitting next to the masked monster.

As the crowd roared, he spun a rare golden fidget on his thumb and all of his spinning minions listened up.

"GREETINGS FIDGETEERS, FIDGETMEN, FIDGET

FIGHTERS, AND GUESTS FROM ACROSS THE UNIVERSE. TONIGHT IS A VERY SPECIAL NIGHT ON PLANET FIDGET. BECAUSE TONIGHT, OUR SPINNERS WILL BE BATTLING FOR THE GOLD..."

As anxious as I was to see Luka, this guy really made me laugh. He sounded like he was breathing into a plastic bag.

"... AS YOU KNOW, THE GOLD TOWER IS WHERE MAGIC HAPPENS. WHATEVER YOU WISH FOR IS YOUR COMMAND ..."

What was he, a genie?

"...BUT THERE WILL BE ONLY ONE GOLDEN SPINNER WINNER. THE MOST POWERFUL, STRONGEST, ENERGETIC SPINNER, STRONG ENOUGH TO BALANCE OUR PLANET BACK ON ITS' AXIS..."

Lies. All lies.

"... SO TINY LILA, LISTEN UP. WIN TONIGHT, AND IT WILL CHANGE YOUR LIFE. YOU WILL BE ABLE TO GET ANYTHING YOU LIKE, FROM SOLARA SPACEPOPS TO ETERNAL E-FI. YOU WILL BE TIMELESS AND IMMORTAL. YOU WILL EXPERIENCE ALL THE UNIVERSE HAS TO OFFER. AND IF YOU LOSE, WELL, YOU LOSE. HAH, HAH!"

The crowd FOOOOED, and spun around and around.

"... TONIGHT'S GOLD MATCH IS EXTRA SPECIAL

BECAUSE THE TWO COMPETING FOR THE GOLD ACTUALLY KNOW EACH OTHER..."

The crowd went wild, "How? How? How?"

"...THEY JUST HAVEN'T SEEN EACH OTHER IN A WHILE. SO LET'S HAVE A REUNION. BRING IN THE SPINNERS!"

Unlike the other levels, this one seemed very simple. They had me just stand in the middle of the arena. There was a dotted circular line drawn around me.

No sign of Luka yet. So I stepped onto the ring first. Step by step, I looked right to left, and then I sensed him, my brother. All that I had to do was grab him and run to the fountain where Mobi would be waiting, but things didn't go as smooth as I had planned.

"GOLD! GOLD! GOLD!"

"FOOO! FOOO! FOOO!"

I was so excited, that I could barely sit still. I had so much to say to him. And then I heard the war drums. FA-FOOM! FA-FOOM! Here we go again. The lights went dim. Oh, what drama.

As I watched my opponent's muscular shadow get closer, I wondered if maybe it wasn't my brother. The Luka I knew was skinny as a string bean. This guy was in great shape. But when he stepped out of the dark and stood right in front of me, it was him. Suddenly I felt like a little kid again. Oh, wait, *I was a little kid.* I had never been so happy to see him.

"Luka, it's me. It's me."

"Who?"

"What do you mean, who?" I said. "It's me, Lila, your sister, we shared the same room till we were 7."

"What are you talking about?" he said. "I don't know you. You twerp."

"Now, stop joking around. Luka, it's me! Lila, your sister! The one who traveled to this crazy planet to rescue you. Who battled three levels to see you."

"Fool. I don't know you."

"Oh, yeah, well I know when you pooped in your pants in 2nd grade. Oh, and that scar on your leg. Remember when you fell off the tree?"

"Lucky guess. You're a joke. Now prepare to be crushed by Luka the Lionater."

"Seriously?" I laughed. "Lionater?"

"You should just go home little girl."

"I'll show you *little girl.*"

When the Captain announced us: LUKA vs. LILA, the spinarium shook. The fans went wild: "GOLD! GOLD! GOLD! GO LILA! GO LILA! GO LIONATOR! GO LIONATOR!"

Luka may have been taller than me, and stronger than me, but I was winning this one to save him.

"FIDGETS READY," Captain Frank said. "SPINERGY SPHERES SET?"

We both said, "Yes."

"FOR THE GOLD. LET THE SPINNING BEGIN."

Suddenly, the circular part of the gold floor we had been standing on started spinning faster and faster and then rose up in the air over 50 feet.

Oh man! I was afraid of heights.

It spun so fast that it was able to float in midair. When I hung my head over the circle edge, I saw a big open circle leading to a red, smoky abyss, and then things got really crazy.

First, 7 steel cylinders shot up from the circular surface, each one carrying a gold fidget on top, and then back down. Up and down. The object of the match was to fetch a fidget and do your tricks as they went up and down. But it wasn't that simple.

Every time you moved, an obstacle presented itself. Like the rising fire stairs, the crazy saw, the random spiking floor, and the kiss of the abyss. Of course, Luka, the risk taker, didn't hesitate to go for the gold, so he was hopping all over the place.

Right away, he did an under the leg. No biggie. But I wasn't the tiny Lila I used to be.

"Take that," I shouted. "You're the nerd. Not me anymore"

I retaliated by doing a Toe Juggle and the Kung Foo Fidgeroo. He fired back with the Head Spin, 10 Toe Drop Shop. I thought he had me there, but then I gave it everything I had. I jumped the stairs and caught every spinner in the air.

"Whoa," he said.

That was the first time I saw fear in his eyes. I was beating him. But beating my brother wasn't the problem. Suddenly, the circle we were on started tilting left and right, making it hard to hold on to, especially when the spikes popped out of the sides and different-sized circles appeared, leading right into the abyss.

"KISS THE ABYSS! KISS THE ABYSS! KISS THE ABYSS!" the fidgeteers cheered.

Just when I thought we had enough, a section of the platform transformed into a trampoline, forcing us to bounce all over the place. And every time I bounced next to Luka, I told him what Lord Spinator was really planning for him.

"You have to trust me Luka," I pleaded. "It's a trick."

"No way, I'm the golden boy."

"All this time, the Spinator has been lying to you, using you for your spinergy. All he wants is power. He's a monster!"

"No way!"

"Luka, I'm your sister. Let's go home. Please?"

And just then, when I took a jump in the air to grab the winning gold fidget key, the platform we were on tipped all the way to the right.

"Oh, no!"

I was spinning on a massive gold disc dangling over the abyss, barely holding on.

When a piece of candy fell out of my pocket, and I didn't hear a thing, I knew I was in trouble.

"Help, somebody!" I screamed.

"*MUAHAHAHAH! HELP YOURSELF!*" Lord Spinator laughed, holding his power remote control from the sidelines, as mischievous Mali snickered by his side.

"Help!" I screamed. My fingertips could barely hold on much longer. As I screamed, nobody came to rescue me. I was so on my own.

My only shot was to get through to my brother. I tried one last time.

"LUKA!!!"

No response. He was too excited about his fool's gold. Getting the golden key was much more important than saving his sister.

"LUKA! HELP ME!"

So he jumped back to grab the key and began running towards the tower. Lord Spinator intervened.

"LUKA, YOU CANNOT BE THE GOLDEN BOY UNTIL YOU TAKE HER POWER. FINISH HER."

He went back and looked down at me just hanging there. My eyes and desperate gaze didn't mean anything.

"FINISH HER! FINISH HER!" Spinator screamed.

And thank God Luka noticed the orange fidget dangling from my neck. It was about to fall off into the abyss. But then Luka froze, his eyes got glassy, and he flashed back.

"Oh, I remember this, Lila, teaching you tricks, blindfolding you."

"Yes! You remember! You told me that I'd know how to do the trick if I ever needed to, that I could do it without seeing, that I could do it just by believing."

"Yes. I remember... You almost killed a cat."

"And when you disappeared, I vowed to never take it off until I found you," I said, "and I never did."

"FINISH HER! FINISH HER!" Lord Spinator insisted.

"I can't believe it's really you," said Luka, finally.

"Yes, it is, Goofball," I laughed. "Now please get me out of here so we can go home."

So Luka pulled me up and placed me to the side, where he knew I'd be safe.

"You're okay now," he said.

Then he looked me in the eyes and said, "I love you sis," but you go home. I'm going for the gold. It's my destiny. I am Luka the Lionater."

I still couldn't believe it. "The Lionater?" Barf.

As he ran away, Spinator went crazy. "FINISH HER!

FINISH HER!" he yelled. "YOU LISTEN TO ME. LUKA! LUKA! YOU BELONG TO ME!"

But Luka wasn't listening to him. He waved his golden key in the air and raced towards the tower. It was located at the edge of the city.

"STOP HIM! STOP HIM!" Lord Spinator yelled at his fidget fighters. "DON'T LET HIM LEAVE!"

But he just kept running and running. He was on a mission for eternal fun and games. And nothing was going to stop him. I was hoping that I could. I didn't travel through a vortex with a farty kid for nothing.

THE GOLDEN TOWER

The tower was way on the other side of the planet. It was at Spinning Cliff. So I ran as fast as I could to stop him, take him to meet my pal Mobi, and spin us both back home to Earth.

"Luka! Luka!," I screamed his name, but he kept on running. I couldn't believe he fell for Spinator's never-ending treasure poop.

When I was 2 blocks away from him I saw him climbing up the Tower stairs.

"Luka, come back," I shouted. "It's a trap. Don't go in!" But my brother didn't listen. He pushed the heavy door open and stepped inside. Seconds later, the door slammed shut behind him. SLAM! I had no idea what was happening to him in there. I thought that would be the last I would see of him. I felt so sad and hopeless. So I just sat on the steps hoping he would come out. Unfortunately, moments later Spinator, Mali and the fidget fighters came out of nowhere. They charged the stairs. But before they went inside after him, Luka was on his way out. There was nothing I could do so I just sat there and listened.

"GOING SOMEWHERE, LUKA? LUKA, MY OLD FRIEND," Lord Spinator asked.

"Hey, where's the candy and video games and free E-fi?" Luka asked. "It's just a dark room with a spinergy-sucking chair. This is all a mistake."

"NO, IT IS NOT."

"But where is my treasure?"

"WHY *YOU* ARE MY TREASURE. *YOU* ARE THE SPINERGY THAT I REQUESTED. AND NOW I HAVE YOURS FOREVER. *FOREVER.* YOU WILL KEEP OUR PLANET ON ITS AXIS AND FEED ME YOUR SPINERGY BECAUSE I AM YOUR LORD SPINATOR! I AM THE MASTER SPINNER OF THE UNIVERSE. *MUAHAHAHAH!*"

"You are a liar Spinator and a mad brainwasher," he said. "I trusted you."

"HA! AND YOU ARE A FOOL ... BUT TO SHOW YOU

THAT I'M NOT ALL *MR. SPINISTER*, I'LL LET YOU STAND OUTSIDE FOR THIS ONE LAST TIME TO SEE THE WONDERFUL LIFE YOU ARE LEAVING BEHIND — BEFORE WE SUCK YOUR SPINERGY DRY. HA! HA! HA!"

I hated the way he was speaking down to my brother. Only I could talk that way to goof ball boy.

I felt so useless just sitting there, so I jumped up, and ran up the stairs to save Luka. I charged Spinator like a little bull.

"Let him go! Let him go! I'm not scared of you!"

"WELL YOU SHOULD BE!" he yelled, slapping me across the cheek, causing my glasses to go flying away.

"Oh no! I can't see!" I screamed, and tumbled down the stairs, right on my butt. "Ow!" How embarrassing.

"Lila, run, go home," Luka yelled. "Get out of here."

"Not without you," I yelled.

"POOR TINY LILA," Spinator said. "LOOKS LIKE YOU'RE NOT RESCUING ANYBODY TODAY... BESIDES, MALI TOLD ME EVERYTHING."

I was doomed. I couldn't see a thing, and I wanted to cry, but then I thought of saving Luka and my friends. They were depending on me. But what could I do? I was just a little girl from Earth. And then I heard a voice...

"When you are ready for the move — the move with no name — you'll know, and you'll be able to do it with your eyes closed." So I knew what I had to do. While they were talking on the steps, I ripped the fidget off my neck, and as I lifted it up to spin it, Lord Spinator laughed,

"OH, CHILD, YOU CAN'T EVEN SEE, AND EVEN IF YOU COULD, YOU COULDN'T SPIN ME."

"*Oh, yes I can.*"

So I shut my eyes and stared at Lord Spinator's pulsating sphere in my mind. Then after I visualized my fidget hitting it right in the center, I took my shot.

"Luka, run," I yelled, as the fidget hit Lord Spinator's

spinergy sphere, right in the center.

"Oh no! What did you do?" Lord Spinator said collapsing onto the ground.

"You did it Lila! You did it!," Luka shouted.

I was thrilled that I did it. I just wished I could've seen it.

A moment later Luka snuck up behind me holding my glasses. "Look what I found."

"Thanks bro."

He even helped me put them on.

Suddenly, the spinergy sphere started to rumble and a burst of colorful spinergy shot out of Spinator in many directions.

"STOP THEM MALI! STOP LUKA! STOP LILA! AND GET YOUR BROTHER MOBI, TOO," he said. "TAKE THE FIDGET FIGHTERS TO CATCH THEM, AND THEN SEND THEM ALL INTO THE ABYSS! AND DO IT NOW! NOW GO!"

As ribbons of his rainbow spinergy spread throughout the city, Lord Spinator couldn't do anything to stop it.

"I COULD HAVE HAD ALL OF THE SPINERGY IN THE ENTIRE UNIVERSE!!!"

"But why did you need it?" I asked.

"WHY? BECAUSE WHEN I WAS A CHILD ON EARTH,

I WAS TAKEN AWAY BY THE FIDGETMEN. I NEVER HAD A CHANCE TO LIVE A NORMAL CHILDHOOD. THEY STOLE MY ENERGY. AND WHEN THEY BROUGHT ME HERE TO MAKE SPINERGY, I GENERATED MORE THAN ANY

FIDGETMAN IN THE PLANET'S HISTORY. AND IT MADE ME FEEL INVINCIBLE..."

I should've asked for the short version.

"...THEN ONCE I GOT A TASTE OF POWER, I WANTED MORE OF IT, SO I KILLED ENERGIVIOS, AND CREATED LORD SPINATOR. I WAS ABOUT TO RULE THE WHOLE UNIVERSE, UNTIL YOU LITTLE EARTHLINGS STOPPED ME."

"Well, Mr. Spinator, that's what you get when you take the best spinners from Earth."

As he collapsed before us, he was breathing heavily. *HUH! HUH! HUH!* Then he started gasping for air. Lord Spinator didn't look so powerful anymore.

I knew Mobi was waiting by the fountain, but I was dying to know who was behind the mask, so I got closer and closer, and I smelled that smell that I hadn't been able to place since I had first arrived. And then it hit me.

"Lila, don't do it," Luka said. "Let's go!"

"I need to know!"

I knew I shouldn't have, but I just couldn't resist. Here goes, I said gently tugging the black mask up. It was stuck.

"C'mon. C'mon."

Inch by inch, I rolled it up from his chin. Yuck, there was

that smell again. As I continued rolling the mask up passed his nose, up to his eyes, I saw a familiar face.

"HOLY PICKLE FARTS!!!"

"Ha-eeh-hah-ha-hah! Lilaaaaaah, so nice to meet again. *Marvelous, just marvelous."*

"Kenny? But, but how? You fell into the abyss."

"Oh, silly Lila."

So he faked his fall into the abyss and had been playing me ever since. But it still didn't make sense. Energivios was hundreds of years old and Kenny was just a boy. How could he be Lord Spinator?

It turned out that he had been immortalized by Captain Frank and the elders of Planet Fidget. But he always needed more spinergy to feel invincible.

"I have been many beings in many lifetimes, but when I need energy, I return to the planet that took mine."

"Kenny, I have one question for you before you disappear for forever. If you had Luka and knew he was the Golden One, why did you come after me?

"Oh Lila, because you were twins. You may have been the one, so I needed both of you. Plus, it was fun showing you around Rotanipsdrol."

Well, all right then. As we stood there, watching the

remainder of his spinergy leave his body, the spinning sirens sounded. The fidget fighters were coming.

"Come on Luka, Mobi is waiting by the fountain, let's go!"

"Wait," I said, bending down to pick my fidget up.

Then, just as I had my fingers on it, Luka pulled me up, pointed to dozens of fidget fighters and shouted "RUN! RUN! RUN!"

ESCAPE FROM PLANET FIDGET

RUN! They were gaining on us. We dodged the spinners for 5 blocks until we arrived at Spincity. "Oh thank gosh." Mobi was at the fountain as planned.

"This is my brother, Luka," she said.

"Nice to meet you," he said. "You'll be back on Earth soon."

"What about my friends and all the others in the abyss?" I asked. "We must save them."

"It's too risky."

"He's right," Luka said

"Well, I'm willing to risk everything," I said. "Besides, we are the two best Spin Masters on the planet. We can spin our way in and out of anything."

Mobi thought about it and nodded okay.

"To the abyss!"

Mobi took us down, deep through the planet's crust to save my friends and all the other kids who had been forced to hold up the planet. But when we got there, these kids didn't look weak. In fact, they looked just the opposite. They were glowing. They had their spinergy back from Lord Spinator.

"Mobi, where is sector 144B?" I asked, and he said, "Follow me."

There was no sign of them. Was I too late? Nope, I just went to the wrong place.

"Monty, Phooey, Beeezly," I yelled at the top of my little lungs, and then I heard them call me.

"Hey Lila," Beeezly said. "Over here! Behind the green spinergy reactor."

"Wow, I'm so happy to see you guys," I said.

"Us too," Monty said.

"I thought you were all drained," I said.

"No way, not me," Beeezly said. "I threw three fidget fighters in a cage."

"What about Flexia and Smartina?"

"Over there," Monty said.

They were drinking a couple of Wecklers in the draining station.

"Okay, cool. Everyone is safe. Now, let's go. We don't have much time. They'll be coming soon."

"Who?"

"Mali and the fidget fighters."

"What about Lord Spinator?"

"He's gone. I drained him, and his last order was for Mali to destroy us. So let's get out of here."

"Are you serious? You drained Lord Spinator?"

"Yes."

"Well. Hooray, Lila! You're our hero!"

They all cheered, and Beeezly lifted me up in the air.

"Thanks, but we have to go now."

"Why?" Monty asked.

Then Beeezly pointed and said, "Uh, oh."

There were tons of fidget fighters coming towards us.

"You mean, Oh no!" Smartina said.

They were getting closer.

So I yelled at the top of my lungs. "GUYS, LET'S GO!"

As we started to run, there were many kids still spinning the planet, barely holding it up. Although they had their spinergy back, they looked frightened and didn't know what to do. So I yelled, "GUYS IF YOU WANT TO GO BACK HOME, GET UP AND FOLLOW US!" So they did. And just in time.

Tons of fidget fighters were coming at us, spinning all over the place, on ramps, on walls, and they were throwing mini fidgets at us. "STOP THEM AT ONCE!" Mali shouted. But these kids weren't stopping. For the first time in a long time they were smiling. They were finally going home. The only problem was that nobody was holding the planet up anymore.

FA-FOOM! FA-FOOM! FA-FOOM!

The whole place started shaking, and everyone was yelling and running for their lives:

"SPINNERQUAKE!"

"SPINNERQUAKE!"

Oh, great.

"SPINNERQUAKE!"

"SPINNERQUAKE!"

We were dodging them the best we could, and then Mobi yelled, "Guys, hurry up! In here."

Together, we pushed a steel door open, but something was preventing us from closing it. It was Mali and her fidget fighters.

"YOU'RE NOT GOING ANYWHERE LUKA AND LILA, EXCEPT TO THE ABYSS OF NO RETURN!" she said. "AND MOBI, DEAR BROTHER, WE COULD'VE BEEN A TEAM.

BUT NOW IT IS TOO LATE. I AM SENTENCING YOU TO BLACK SPINNERLAND FOR FRETERNITY."

Then she pointed to her fidget fighters and said, "TAKE THEM NOW. AND LEAVE THE OTHERS."

Then just as the fidget fighters started to grab Phooey, one of the kids who had been spinning the planet yelled, "Watch out," and he slammed four fidgets on the ground as hard as he could. BOOM! BOOM! BOOM! BOOM!

Suddenly, thousands of ball-bearings shot all over the place like marbles, and Mali and all the fidget fighters couldn't stand still. They lost control and spun around in circles. Then one by one, they fell down into the abyss.

"Clever move, Danny," Mobi said. "Clever move."

"Wait, did you just say Danny?" I yelled.

It was Daredevil Danny.

"I don't believe it, you're alive."

"Yea, they didn't drain me completely."

"Well, let's talk about that back home," I said. "You have a furry earthling named Bosco who's going crazy without you."

Mobi explained that leaving Planet Fidget was different than arriving. Now, instead of staring into a little fidget, thousands of kids from across the universe were going to be able to stare into a giant spiral. He wasn't kidding.

Mobi led us to a room with a gigantic round bathtub.

"It's called a Spinnerfall," he said

When I looked into it, there were tons of beautiful colors spinning around and around. It created a really cool spiral. It looked similar to a fidget spinning, except the rings were huge. They definitely led to somewhere. Another vortex?

I whispered to Luka, "Looks like a giant toilet bowl." He laughed. "Someone is going to have to flush us home." It was good to have my moronic brother back.

"Okay guys, now pay close attention," Mobi said. "The most important part of going home is thinking about where you live. You need to focus and imagine yourself there, because if you don't you could end up anywhere, and there are much meaner villains out there than Lord Spinator."

This whole thing sounded crazy, but after what I had witnessed over the past few days or months, I was ready for anything. Mobi had all the kids line up, and he said, "Brothers and sisters of the universe, when I say jump, you jump, and you jump fast because nobody is holding the planet up anymore. That means that if you don't escape now, you'll be spinning into a never-ending black fidget hole. And then you're on your own.

READY. SET. SPIRAL.

One after another, the kids jumped, hopefully remembering what planet they were from. Before we jumped, Luka and I gave our favorite fidgeteer a hug.

"What about you?" I asked.

"I am a fidgeteer. I've always been a fidgeteer," Mobi said, "I can't abandon the planet. I'm staying with Captain Frank."

As Luka and I had tears in our eyes, Mobi said. "Hey, I never showed you the invisible Fidgetship, did I?"

We both shook our heads and said, "No."

"Well maybe I'll show you sometime," he said, winking.

"Now jump into the portal. Hurry up."

All I remember was swirling around with all types of creatures. Some blue kid's tail kept poking me in the head, and there was a yellow guy with six noses. I could've sworn there were a few fidget fighters swirling around in there too. I prayed not.

I felt like I was traveling back in time and then back into the future. There was also a lot of screaming and growling and screeching. My face stretched out like putty. It was one heck of a flight. And then it just stopped. I smelled popcorn, my skin itched, and I heard a buzz. When I opened my eyes, we were lying on a grass field about 10 blocks from our house. We had no idea what day or year it was, but things looked pretty much the same. People were walking dogs, riding bikes, flying kites, and little kids were swinging high in the sky.

We were both in such shock that we didn't say a word. But I'm sure he was thinking the same thing as me: What in the world just happened to us? We had no idea what to do next. We certainly couldn't tell anybody. They wouldn't have believed us — especially our parents. We had no idea how that was going to go. Did they think we ran away? Or worse?

Were they 100 years old now? Who knew? After much thought, we showed up at dinnertime. We didn't bother ringing the bell.

"Mom, Dad, we're home."

Here it comes. *Oh, my God, you're alive?*

Nope, not the case. Instead, my mom said. "So did you have fun at Melanie's house last night?"

"Last night?"

"Yeah, you think we didn't sneak out of the house when we were kids?"

"And Luka, we know where you've been. Playing fidgets with your troublemaker friends."

We just stood there in disbelief as Lilo licked my feet. We couldn't believe they thought we had only been gone for one day. It had felt like months or more.

"Sorry," we both said, we won't do it again."

As we were walking away home free, my mom said, "Excuse me, Lila."

"Yes," I said.

"What is that on your neck?"

"Oh, this? It's a fidget."

"I didn't think you were into that type of thing. You're much too smart for that. I thought that was more Luka's thing."

I wasn't letting her put him down anymore.

"Well, you know Luka's thing is a very smart thing. You just don't understand it. But I do, and it's *AWESOME!* You should have him teach you a trick or two. But I don't know if you could do one. It takes coordination, and patience."

She frowned.

"Who knows, one day a little girl might use it to save thousands of kids from a mad man on another planet?"

"Oh please," she laughed. "Now go wash your hands. It's meatball night."

Meatball night. Me and Luka laughed behind her back. "I'm being poisoned," I whispered. It was like we never left. That night, we sat on the steps staring up at the stars munching on chocolate bars. But something was different.

Far, far away, across galaxies, there was a black hole in the shape of a fidget.

"Well, it's good to have you back, goofball," I said.

"You too, nerd face," Luka said. "Hey, by the way, congrats."

"For what?"

"You're a Master Spinner now. You're a hero, sis. My hero. You saved all of those kids. On Earth and on thousands of other planets. "

After a brief moment of silence, I smiled and said, "Sure wish we had a couple of Wecklers." Then when our eyes could no longer stay open, we went to sleep in our own beds.

WANNA SPIN AGAIN?
ONE MONTH LATER

As time moved on, Luka and I talked less about our fidget adventure. Then one afternoon out of nowhere Luka asked me if Kenny's treehouse was real.

"Of course," I said. "You wanna see it?"

"Well do you know where it is?"

"I think so. Just bring some boots, a hairnet, bug spray, and a jar of pickles."

"Pickles?"

That was a joke between me and Kenny, or *Lord Spinator*. So we went under the fence, into the sludge, through the woods, just past the creek, and when we walked through the swarm of mosquitos, we were there.

"Holy moly," I said, pointing to the sign on the tree.
It read: ROTANIPSDROL

But it was a code written backwards: LORD SPINATOR

"So obvious! How did I miss that?"

"Cool," Luka said. "But looks like an ordinary tree house."

"Yes it does. Now take your shoes off."

"You're kidding me, right?"

When I opened the door, everything was the way we had left it before the take off.

"Holy moly!" Luka shouted.

There were the fidgets hanging from the ceiling. And there was the telescope. We took a peek and of course it was pointed exactly at the black hole in space. And last but not least, there was the intergalactic tracker. I showed him how it worked as best as I could. Fortunately, the video that showed Luka being taken away in the library was on the tablet screen.

"Hey, that's me," he said.

"It sure is goofball."

We sat down for a while talking about our trip to Planet Fidget, about Mobi. Sometimes it still feels like it was a dream.

Then when we were about to leave, we both heard something. A buzzing sound. So we slowly turned our heads to see what is was.

And there on the table was a shiny golden fidget, and it was spinning all by itself.

As our eyes widened we looked at each other, walked over to the table, sat down and stared.

We smiled at the same time, and we both said:

"WANNA SPIN AGAIN?"

METIN SOZEN is an Art Director, Graphic Designer and Illustrator. He has been working in advertising for over 10 years in Istanbul, Atlanta, Minneapolis, and New York City.

Metin's work has received recognition from The One Club, The Art Directors Club of New York, Communication Arts, The Andy's, Graphis, AdFed of Minnesota, How magazine and Print magazine.

Metin lives in Sleepy Hollow, NY with his wife, two children and a cat named Kedi which means "cat" in Turkish.

BRUCE GOLDSTEIN is the Author of the best-selling book, "Puppy Chow is Better than Prozac." It's been published in the US, Italy, and China, and received praise from The NY Post, The Morning Show, Publisher's Weekly, and best-selling Author, James Patterson.

Bruce has also worked over 20 years as a Copywriter and Creative Director at many NY ad agencies, including Chiat/Day, Deutsch, and AKQA.

Goldstein received a B.F.A. in Advertising Design from The Fashion Institute of Technology in 1992. He lives in Manhattan with his wife, two children, and a hamster named Peanut.

For the latest adventures of Luka and Lila visit
escapefromplanetfidget.com

#escapefromplanetfidget